Dear Parent:

Congratulations! Your child is
the first steps on an exciting j
The destination? Independent

STEP INTO READING® will help your child get there. The program offers
books at five levels that accompany children from their first attempts at
reading to reading success. Each step includes fun stories, fiction and
nonfiction, and colorful art. There are also Step into Reading Sticker Books,
Step into Reading Math Readers, Step into Reading Write-In Readers, Step into
Reading Phonics Readers, and Step into Reading Phonics First Steps! Boxed
Sets—a complete literacy program with something to interest every child.

Learning to Read, Step by Step!

Ready to Read Preschool–Kindergarten
• big type and easy words • rhyme and rhythm • picture clues
For children who know the alphabet and are eager to
begin reading.

Reading with Help Preschool–Grade 1
• basic vocabulary • short sentences • simple stories
For children who recognize familiar words and sound out
new words with help.

Reading on Your Own Grades 1–3
• engaging characters • easy-to-follow plots • popular topics
For children who are ready to read on their own.

Reading Paragraphs Grades 2–3
• challenging vocabulary • short paragraphs • exciting stories
For newly independent readers who read simple sentences
with confidence.

Ready for Chapters Grades 2–4
• chapters • longer paragraphs • full-color art
For children who want to take the plunge into chapter books
but still like colorful pictures.

STEP INTO READING® is designed to give every child a successful
reading experience. The grade levels are only guides. Children can progress
through the steps at their own speed, developing confidence in their
reading, no matter what their grade.

Remember, a lifetime love of reading starts with a single step!

The Disney Fairies Story Collection

Step into Reading, Random House, and the Random House colophon are registered trademarks
of Random House, Inc.

Visit us on the Web!
www.stepintoreading.com
www.randomhouse.com/kids

Educators and librarians, for a variety of teaching tools, visit us at
www.randomhouse.com/teachers

Library of Congress Cataloging-in-Publication Data
The Disney fairies story collection.
    v. cm.
"Step 3 and Step 4 Books; A Collection of Three Early Readers."
Contents: A game of hide-and-seek — The great fairy race — The fairy berry bake-off —
Meet the fairies!
ISBN 978-0-7364-2710-4 (pbk.)

PZ7.D62453 2010
[E]—dc22
2009016493

MANUFACTURED IN CHINA   10 9 8 7 6 5 4 3 2

The Disney Fairies Story Collection

Step 3 and Step 4 Books

A Collection of Three Early Readers

Random House New York

Contents

Disney fairies

A Game of Hide-and-Seek

By Tennant Redbank

Illustrated by the Disney Storybook Artists

Random House New York

Pixie Hollow was quiet and still.

No fairy wings fluttered.

No fairy voices filled the air.

Where had all the fairies gone?

Suddenly,

along came Tinker Bell.

She flew alone

over a garden.

Tink pulled up close
to a tall tulip.

Rosetta peeked out
from behind some petals.
They were playing a game
of fairy hide-and-seek.
And Tinker Bell was IT!

Tinker Bell still had
so many fairies to find.
There were Rani and Bess,
Nettle and Fira,
Dulcie and Terence,
Silvermist, Iridessa, and Fawn.
Beck was usually easy to spot.
She couldn't stay still for long.
But Prilla was very good
at hide-and-seek.
It might take Tink a while
to find her.

Tinker Bell looked behind
a spiderweb.

She checked under a pinecone.

She peeked into a knothole.

Then she saw a bright light.

It was shining from

behind a leaf.

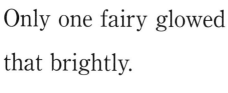

Only one fairy glowed

that brightly.

"Fira!" Tink yelled.

Tink pulled the leaf back.

There she was!

"You found me!"

Fira said, giggling.

Tink couldn't stay to talk.

She had other fairies to find!

Tink flew over the meadow.

She stopped short.

She sniffed the air.

She smelled lemons.

Tink followed her nose . . .

right to Dulcie,

a baking-talent fairy.

Dulcie was hiding

near a patch of clover.

The lemon cake she had baked

that morning gave her away!

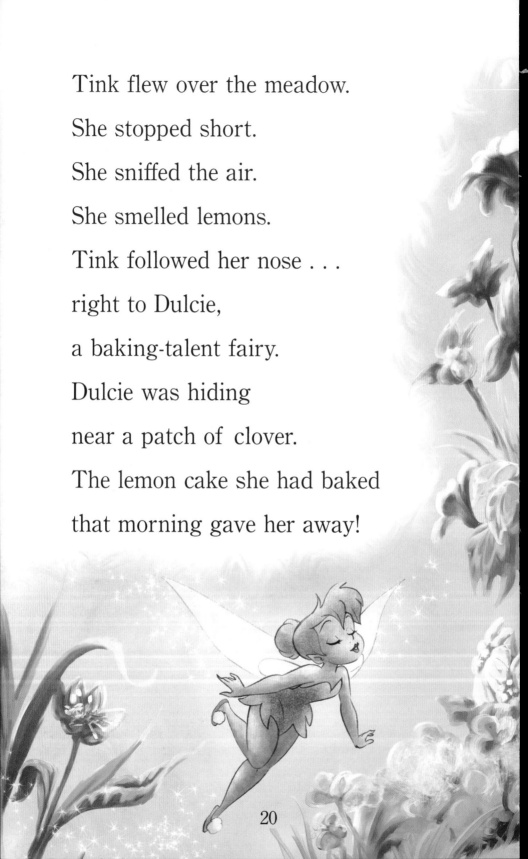

Tink left the meadow
and started searching again.
Bright blue footprints
crossed her path.
The footprints led
over some pebbles
and down to the river.
There Tink saw Bess
hiding among the pussy willows.

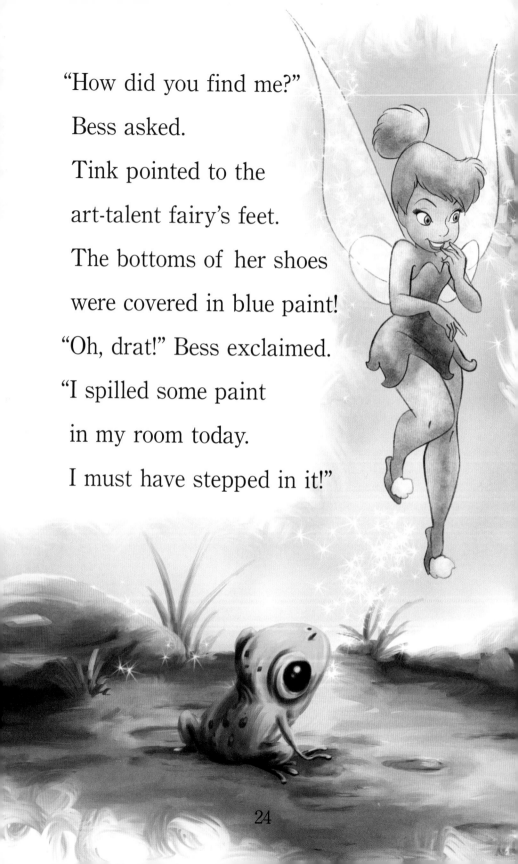

"How did you find me?"
Bess asked.

Tink pointed to the
art-talent fairy's feet.
The bottoms of her shoes
were covered in blue paint!

"Oh, drat!" Bess exclaimed.

"I spilled some paint
in my room today.
I must have stepped in it!"

Tink found Silvermist
behind a rainspout.

She spotted Fawn
in a bird's nest.

Iridessa was trying to blend in
with the fireflies.

Nettle was hiding
in an old cocoon.

Tinker Bell still had not found
all her friends.
She flew to the Mermaid Lagoon.
There she saw water flowing
from a large stone
sitting on dry ground.

Tink fluttered around the stone.

On the other side,

she found Rani,

a water-talent fairy.

Rani was playing

with a water ball.

"I got you!" Tink shouted.

Rani jumped.

She was startled.

She dropped the water ball.

It burst into a hundred droplets.

Then Rani pulled all the drops

back together again.

She threw the water ball at Tink.

Tink sprang out of the way.

"Hey!" Tink yelled.

"We're playing hide-and-seek,

not fairy tag!"

Tink had a game to finish,
so she flew into the woods.
"I can't believe
I haven't found Beck," she said.
Up ahead, she saw
a flash of color.
Tink flew closer.
It was a red-spotted toadstool.
But wait . . .
something was behind it.
Maybe it was Beck!

It wasn't Beck.

But it was a

red-haired fairy in a green cap.

"Prilla!" Tink shouted.

Tink told Prilla
who she had already found.
Then Prilla cried out,
"Tink, look!"
A beetle floated
right in front of their noses—
upside down!
It sparkled with fairy dust.

Tink and Prilla followed
the trail of fairy dust.
Fairy dust makes
fairies fly—and beetles, too!
They flew until they saw
a silly sight.
Terence, a fairy-dust-talent
sparrow man,
was trying
to pull beetles
from the air.

"Tink, Prilla, help!"

Terence cried.

"I was hiding in a little hole.

A bunch of beetles found me and

got into my bag of fairy dust!"

Prilla stayed to help Terence.

Tink still had more fairies to find.

Who was left?

Tink settled on a lily pad
to think for a bit.
She had found Terence and Prilla,
Fawn, Iridessa, Rosetta,
Nettle and Silvermist,
Dulcie, Rani, Fira, and Bess.
The only fairy
she had not found was . . .
Beck!

Tink flew off again.

She looked and looked.

Then she asked

the other fairies for help.

They all joined in.

They explored every garden.

They searched over the meadow

and the lagoon

and the fairy-dust mill.

Where in Pixie Hollow was Beck?

Tink tugged at her bangs.
She was stumped!
Beck was usually
the easiest fairy to find.
Today Beck was not just
an animal-talent fairy—
she was a master hider!

Tink was about to yell
"Come on out, Beck!"
But before she did,
a soft sound reached her ears.
It seemed like a breath.
Or a whisper.
Or . . . a snore!

Tink followed the noise.

It was coming from a hollow log.

She poked her head inside.

There she found

Beck curled up

with a family of hedgehogs!

"Wake up, sleepyhead!" Tink sang out.

Beck opened her eyes and yawned.

"You found me already?"

Beck asked.

"Already?" Tink cried.

"I've been looking for hours!

Beck, you are the last

hide-and-seek fairy!"

"I am?" Beck asked.

"How nice!"

She rolled over.

She snuggled back in

with the hedgehogs.

Soon Beck was asleep again.

Tink sighed.

Beck and the hedgehogs

looked so cozy.

Tink pushed Beck over a little.

She was tired after

all that looking.

Maybe a little nap . . .

only for a minute or two . . .

Just before Tink's eyes closed,

she heard a voice call,

"Tink? Beck?

Where are you?"

Another game of

fairy hide-and-seek had begun!

The Great Fairy Race

By Tennant Redbank

Illustrated by the Disney Storybook Artists

Random House New York

"On your marks!"

Queen Clarion called.

"Get set. . . ."

She raised her hands in the air.

"Go!" Queen Clarion shouted.

A light flashed across the sky.

The Great Fairy Race was on!

The rules of the Great Fairy Race
were simple.
The first one to cross the finish
line was the winner.
But the fairies could not
use their own feet or wings.
No running.
No flying.

Beck rode a squirrel.
Right behind her
was Fawn on a frog.
Rani flew through the air
on Brother Dove's back.

Fira soared
in a balloon.

Silvermist surfed on a wave.

Tinker Bell

rode a machine

she had made

out of pots and pans.

And Lily sat high atop
a giant snail.
"Hurry, Lily," Bess called,
"or you will come in last!"
Lily laughed.
"I don't care," she said.
"I like the view up here."

"Coming through!"

Silvermist yelled.

She sailed past Beck.

Now she was first!

But then Fawn's frog
made a mighty jump.
He hopped
right over Silvermist!

"This fairy race is all mine!"
Fawn crowed.

"Not for long," Rani said.
She passed Fawn
from above.

Lily was far behind the others.

But she didn't mind.

She even stopped

to water a flower

next to the path.

"I'll get there soon enough,"

she said.

The fairies crossed the stream.

They tore through the meadow.

They rounded the Home Tree.

They zoomed past the gardens.

But fairy after fairy
ran into trouble.
Beck's squirrel saw
another squirrel.
He ran off to play.

"Turn around!"

Beck cried in Squirrel.

"We're going the wrong way!"

The squirrel scampered up a tree.

Beck was stuck going with him!

Fawn laughed at Beck.
But then her frog
spotted a fat fly
over the pond.

Splash!
Before she knew it,
Fawn and the frog
were in the pond.
The frog was happy.
Fawn was not.

"See you at the finish line!"

Tink called to Fawn.

A minute later,
the wheels of Tink's machine
got stuck in the mud.
"I'll never win now!"
Tink moaned.

Fira's balloon sprang a leak.
It took Fira ten minutes
to fix the hole.

Poor Bess got lost.

She knew she was somewhere

between the mossy rocks

and the crooked tree.

But where?

She took a map

out of her pocket.

"Which way?"

she asked herself.

Rani saw a pretty waterfall.
She stopped to look at it
and fell behind.

Silvermist was not watching
where she was headed.
She sailed into a spiderweb
and got stuck.

Before long,

Beck and Fawn had their animals

under control.

Tink dug out her machine.

Bess found her way.

Rani and Silvermist

were on track again.

"I see the end!"

Fira yelled.

They raced for the finish line.

They were neck and neck,

and wing to wing.

Who was going to be first?

Who would win

the Great Fairy Race?

The fairies put on
a last burst of speed.
They were almost there. . . .

All of a sudden,

Tink's front wheel

ran over the squirrel's tail!

Tink and Beck

and the squirrel went down.

"Nuts and bolts!"

Tink groaned.

Fawn and her frog
were right behind them.
They could not stop!
Fawn's frog jumped and tripped.
It bumped into
Rani and Brother Dove.

Brother Dove crashed into
Fira's balloon.
The balloon lost air
and headed for the ground.

Bess and Silvermist
went down, too.

Not one of the fairies

made it across the finish line.

But wait!

Slowly, slowly,

Lily and her snail inched forward.

They passed Bess.

"Are you taking a rest, Bess?"

Lily asked.

Lily and her snail
passed Fira.
They passed Rani and Tink
and Beck and Fawn
and Silvermist.
"So who won the race?"
Lily asked.

Then Lily and her giant snail
crossed the finish line!

"Lily is the winner!"

Queen Clarion cried.

"I am?" Lily asked.

Lily looked with surprise
at the other fairies.
"I thought the race
was already over,"
she said.

The fairies cheered for Lily.
"Hooray for Lily
and her snail!"
everyone called.

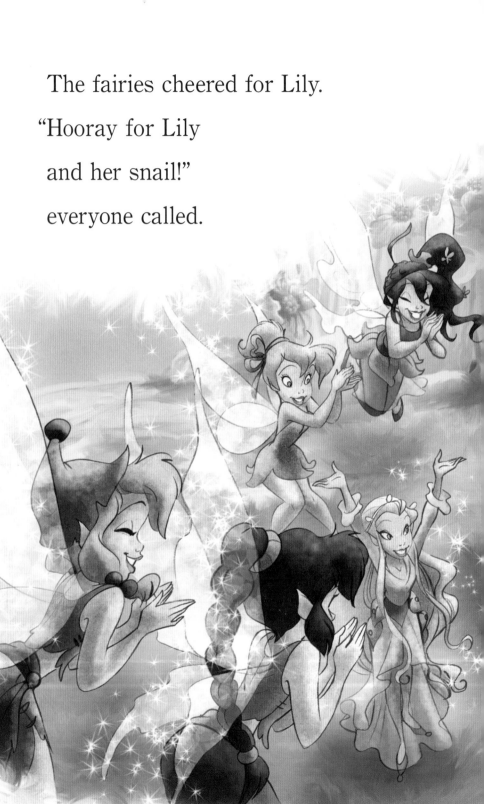

Queen Clarion put a necklace
of flowers around Lily's neck.
She put one around
the snail's neck, too.

"Who knew
a snail would be
the fastest creature
in Pixie Hollow?"
Queen Clarion said.

The
Fairy Berry Bake-Off

DISNEP fairies

By Daisy Alberto

Illustrated by the Disney Storybook Artists

Random House 🏠 New York

All over Pixie Hollow, the Never
fairies were hard at work. Each fairy
had a talent and a special job to do.

The garden-talent fairy Lily was
in her garden, watering the seedlings.

The art-talent fairy Bess was in
her studio, working on a new
painting.

The water-talent fairy Silvermist was collecting dewdrops.

The light-talent fairy Fira was training the fireflies to light Pixie Hollow at night.

The animal-talent fairy Beck was
helping a lost baby chipmunk find
his way home.

And Tinker Bell, a pots-and-pans
fairy, was in her workshop, fixing a
broken frying pan.

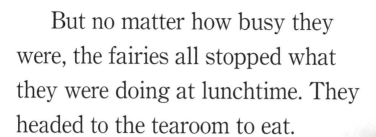

But no matter how busy they were, the fairies all stopped what they were doing at lunchtime. They headed to the tearoom to eat.

The tearoom was one of the most popular places in Pixie Hollow. It was peaceful. It was pretty. And best of all, the food was yummy!

The fairies gathered there every day for all of their meals.

"I wonder what tasty treats the baking-talent fairies will have for us today," said Lily.

"Maybe we'll have whole roasted cherries with cinnamon glaze," replied Bess.

"Yum!" exclaimed Tink. "I'm so hungry, I could eat a whole cherry all by myself."

The other fairies laughed. They couldn't wait to find out what was for lunch.

Strawberry soup, nutmeg pie, blackberry cake, and roasted walnuts stuffed with figs—every fairy had a favorite dish!

There were so many wonderful treats, Tinker Bell couldn't decide what to try first. At that moment, something special caught her eye. She popped a tiny tart into her mouth.

"That's the best tart I've ever had!" she said.

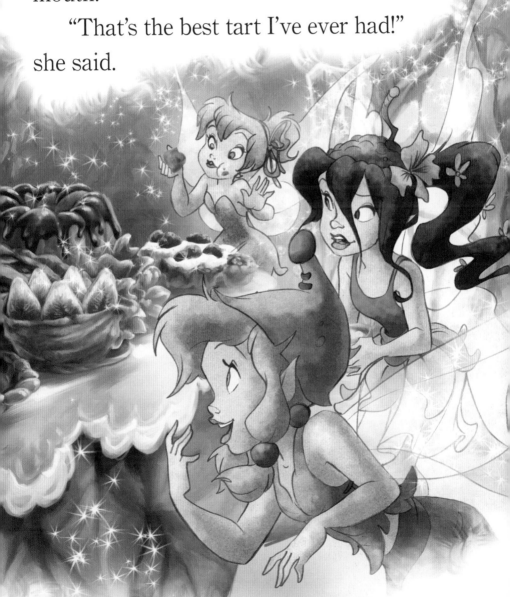

In the kitchen, Dulcie, a baking-talent fairy, overheard Tink. "Tinker Bell loves my tarts!" she exclaimed with a smile.

Dulcie was proud of her baking. She always tried to make the fluffiest rolls, the flakiest pies, and the creamiest frosting. She really loved to bake. But she also loved to watch the other fairies enjoy her tasty treats.

The baking-talent fairy Ginger was nearby. When she heard Dulcie, she frowned.

"I think that was one of *my* tarts," she told Dulcie.

"Oh, I don't think so," Dulcie said sweetly. "Your tarts tend to be a little dry and hard."

Ginger most certainly did not agree. She knew that her tarts were always moist and flaky.

The next day, Dulcie baked
blueberries with fresh whipped
cream. The fairies ate every last one.

"Yum!" said Tink. "Are there
any more?"

Dulcie blushed. She beamed.

"They love my baking!" she said
proudly.

Dulcie wanted to be the best
baking-talent fairy in all of Pixie
Hollow.

Back in the kitchen, Dulcie peeked into the oven. She saw Ginger's gingerbread.

"It looks a little flat," she said. "You should follow my recipe, Ginger. My gingerbread is much fluffier."

Ginger had had enough of Dulcie's bragging.

"My gingerbread is perfect," she said.

"No, it isn't. But don't feel bad," said Dulcie. "Some fairies just need more practice than others."

That did it! Ginger was fed up.

"Dulcie, you wouldn't know what to do with a berry if it fell into your piecrust!" said Ginger.

"Ha!" said Dulcie. "I could outbake you any day!"

"Prove it," said Ginger.

"You're on!" cried Dulcie.

The fairy berry bake-off began.
Ginger and Dulcie were going to
prove once and for all who was
the best baker. It was a battle
neither fairy wanted to lose.

That evening, Ginger made
boysenberry custard served in a vanilla
bean. Dulcie made her magic blackberry
turnovers.

"Wow!" said Tink. "They really
do turn over!"

The next day, Ginger made her
famous five-berry crumble. The
fairies cleaned their plates and licked
every last crumb from their spoons.

Dulcie peeked into the tearoom.
"Hmmph," she said. "Wait until
they try *mine*."

Dulcie carried her right-side-up upside-down cake into the tearoom and proudly placed it on a table. The fairies didn't even notice. They were too busy finishing Ginger's five-berry crumble.

Dulcie couldn't believe it.

"Don't you like my cake?" she asked the fairies.

"It looks wonderful," said Tink. "But we're full."

Dulcie frowned. "How about just a little taste?" she pleaded.

The fairies shook their heads. They patted their stomachs.

"We couldn't eat another bite," Bess said.

Ginger grinned. It looked like
she had won this round of the berry
bake-off.

Dulcie knew she needed to make something extra-special for the next meal. So for lunch the following day, she outdid herself.

There were puddings and pies. There were crumpets and cakes. There were piles of Tink's favorite cream puffs.

The fairies ate and ate until they couldn't eat any more. Dulcie's feast was a hit.

But the berry bake-off was only getting started.

The next day at breakfast, Dulcie and Ginger waited in the tearoom for the fairies to arrive.

"Try a muffin," Dulcie said to Tink. "They are soft and sweet."

"How about a honey bun?" asked Ginger. "They're even softer and sweeter."

"No, a muffin!" said Dulcie.

"A bun!" cried Ginger.

"Er, I'm not hungry," said Tink, flying away.

Dulcie and Ginger didn't even notice that Tink had left. They kept arguing.

The fairies worked hard all
morning. They were looking forward
to a nice, relaxing lunch. Dulcie and
Ginger met them as they entered the
tearoom.

Dulcie waved a spoon. "Taste this!" she called out.

"No, taste this!" shouted Ginger. "Mine's better!"

But none of the fairies stopped. The tearoom no longer seemed very relaxing at all!

Back in the kitchen, things were no better.

"Get me an egg!" Dulcie shouted to an egg-collecting fairy.

"I need more flour!" Ginger snapped at a kitchen-talent sparrow man.

One by one, the other fairies left
the kitchen. They didn't want to be
around Dulcie and Ginger. The berry
bake-off was getting out of control.

Soon Dulcie and Ginger were
alone in the kitchen. But they didn't
notice. They were both too busy.

They sifted and stirred. They
mixed and measured. They each
wanted their next dessert
to be their best.

Ginger made fresh raspberry cupcakes with vanilla cream filling. She used the finest raspberries that grew in Pixie Hollow.

Dulcie made her special seven-layer cake, with six kinds of berries.

Dulcie reached for a berry to top off her cake.

"That's *my* berry!" Ginger exclaimed. "You can't have it."

"It's *my* berry," Dulcie replied. "I'm sure of it."

"It's mine!" said Ginger. She grabbed the berry.

"No, it's mine!" said Dulcie. She held on tight.

Neither fairy wanted to give in. They pulled and pulled, until . . .

. . . Dulcie stumbled backward—
right into her cake!

Ginger stumbled backward, too.
Her cupcakes went flying
everywhere!

"Oops!" said both fairies at once.

One cupcake hit Dulcie. Another hit Ginger.

Just then, Tink walked in to see what all the fuss was about. A flying cupcake landed right on her head.

"Hey!" cried Tink. "What is going on here?"

Dulcie and Ginger looked
around. The kitchen was a disaster.
Cake and cupcakes were everywhere!
"Oh, no!" said Dulcie.
"What have we done?" cried
Ginger.

They rushed over to Tink.

Tink was mad. "The berry bake-off has gone too far," she said. "Don't you understand that you are both great bakers?"

Dulcie and Ginger blushed. They looked at each other. Could it be true? Could they *both* be great bakers?

Dulcie brushed Ginger's cupcake crumbs off her apron. She tasted her fingers.

"Oh, my," said Dulcie. "This is good!"

"Really?" asked Ginger.

"Yes!" said Dulcie.

Ginger smiled. She took a tiny taste of Dulcie's seven-layer cake.

"Wow," she said. "So is yours!"

"Why don't you bake together?" Tink suggested.

And so the fairy berry bake-off
ended in a tasty tie.

Meet the Fairies!

Hi, I'm Tink!

Talent: Tinkering

Best friends: Rani, Prilla

I like: Fixing things, adventures

Favorite food: Pumpkin muffins

Favorite flower: Silver bell

Hi, I'm Silvermist!

Talent: Shaping water

Best friends: Iridessa, Rani

I like: When everyone gets along

Favorite food: Water chestnuts

Favorite flower: Water lily

Hi, I'm Bess!

Talent: Painting

Best friends: Lily, Violet

I like: Sharing my work with others

Favorite food: Blueberry pie

Favorite flower: Tulip

Hi, I'm Beck!

Talent: Speaking to animals

Best friends: Fawn, Mother Dove, Fira

I like: Playing with baby animals, caring for Mother Dove

Favorite food: Acorn pancakes

Favorite flower: Dandelion

Hi, I'm Lily!

Talent: Gardening

Best friends: Iris, Bess, Rosetta

I like: Spending time with my plants, going possum-fern spotting

Favorite food: Everfruit

Favorite flower: I love them all!

Hello, I'm Queen Clarion!

Talent: Ruling over Pixie Hollow

Best friend: I love all fairies equally.

I like: Peace and prosperity

Favorite food: Fig-chocolate cake

Favorite flower: Calla lily